© 2007, Disney Enterprises, Inc.
Published by Hachette Partworks Ltd
ISBN: 978-1-906965-18-1
Date of Printing: June 2009
Printed in Singapore by Tien Wah Press

Long ago, beneath the shimmering stars of a desert night, a fantastic tale began to unfold.

Jafar, adviser to the Sultan of Agrabah, was searching for a lamp hidden in a place known as the Cave of Wonders. This magical lamp held within it a powerful Genie who could grant three wishes to whoever possessed the lamp.

The only way to find the entrance to the Cave of Wonders was to match two halves of a scarab medallion. The evil Jafar had one half. Now he and his parrot, Iago, waited for a thief named Gazeem to bring the other. Suddenly they heard the muffled sound of galloping hooves. Moments later Gazeem's horse skidded to a halt.

"Have you brought it?" asked Jafar.

"I have, O Patient One," answered Gazeem.

Jafar took out his half of the medallion and put
the two pieces together. The scarab began to glow.
Then it sprang from Jafar's hand and streaked
across the desert like a shooting star!

"Follow the trail!" Jafar shouted as he spurred
his horse.

The two men followed the enchanted scarab until
it split into two lights in a dune. The dune grew
larger and larger. Finally it transformed itself into
the face of a huge tiger, with two glowing eyes.

"At last, the Cave of Wonders!" cried Jafar. He
turned to Gazeem. "Now remember, bring me the
lamp. The rest of the treasure is yours, but the lamp
is mine."

Trembling, Gazeem entered the tiger's mouth. In an instant its huge jaws clamped shut around him.

"Only one may enter here!" thundered the Voice of the Cave. "Seek thee out the Diamond in the Rough." With that the cave sank back into the sand, leaving only the scarab behind.

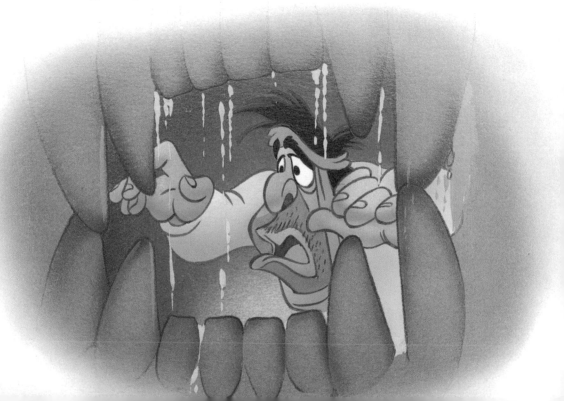

"I can't believe it! We'll never get that stupid lamp now!" squawked Iago after he had retrieved the scarab.

"Patience, Iago," said Jafar. He thought for a moment. "The 'Diamond in the Rough'. Someone poor and ragged on the outside, but pure and noble on the inside. I must find this one," he said with an evil smile.

The next morning in Agrabah's marketplace, a young man named Aladdin and his monkey, Abu, were helping themselves to breakfast. The fruit seller saw them and sent Razoul, the Sultan's chief guard, after them. "Stop, thief!" shouted Razoul as they raced away.

The guards chased Aladdin and Abu through the streets, but they managed to escape. As they sat down to eat, Aladdin noticed two hungry children. Like him, they had no money for food. So, although he was starving himself, Aladdin gave his food to the grateful children.

Inside the palace the Sultan was having a difficult morning, too. His beautiful daughter, Princess Jasmine, had insulted yet another prince who had come to propose to her.

"Oh, Jasmine, you've got to stop rejecting every prince who comes to call," said the Sultan. "The law says you must marry a prince by your next birthday."

"The law is wrong. If I do marry, I want it to be for love," replied Jasmine.

Later, as Jasmine petted her tiger, she said softly, "I've never had any real friends – except you, Rajah. I've never even been outside these palace walls. I must get away before it's too late."

That night Jasmine changed into ordinary clothes. With a sad goodbye to Rajah, she climbed over the garden wall to freedom.

Jasmine's eyes grew wide with wonder as she
explored the marketplace of Agrabah the next
morning. She had never seen so many strange
sights before.

Soon Jasmine spotted a hungry child. Without a second thought she plucked an apple from a fruit stand and handed it to him.

"You'd better be able to pay for that!" shouted the fruit seller.

"I'm sorry, sir," stammered the Princess. "I don't have any money. But if you let me go to the palace, I can get some from the Sultan."

"Thief!" shouted the fruit seller.

Luckily for Jasmine, Aladdin came by just in time.

"Forgive my poor sister," he said to the fruit seller. "She's a little crazy in the head. She thinks the monkey is the Sultan."

As the fruit seller thought this over, Aladdin and Jasmine disappeared into the crowd.

Aladdin led Jasmine to his rooftop home. "We're safe here," he said. "Where do you come from?"

"I ran away from home," replied Jasmine, "and I'm never going back. My father is forcing me to get married."

"That's awful!" Aladdin exclaimed.

Suddenly Jasmine's eyes met Aladdin's, and they leaned towards one another to kiss.

   Meanwhile, in his secret laboratory high above
the palace, Jafar consulted his magic hourglass.
   "Oh, Sands of Time!" he chanted. "Reveal to me
the one who can enter the Cave of Wonders." The
sand parted, and gradually an image began to
appear. It was the image of Aladdin!
   Jafar turned to Iago and flashed his evil grin.
"Let's have the guards extend him an invitation to
the palace, shall we?"

Just as Jasmine and Aladdin were about to kiss, the guards arrived. Aladdin ran to the edge of the roof and held out his hand to Jasmine.

"Do you trust me?" he asked. She nodded.

"Then jump!" he cried. They landed safely in a pile of hay, but before they could get away, Razoul grabbed them.

Angrily Jasmine threw back her hood. "Unhand him, by order of the Princess!" she commanded.

"The Princess?" repeated Aladdin in surprise.

"I cannot release this prisoner," said Razoul. "The orders for his arrest come from Jafar."

Jasmine rushed back to the palace. "The guards just took a boy from the marketplace on your orders," she scolded Jafar. "I want him released at once!"

"I'm sorry, Princess, but he has already been executed," said Jafar.

"No! How could you?" cried Jasmine. In tears, she ran to her room. "It's all my fault," she sobbed to Rajah. "He was so gentle and brave. I didn't even know his name."

But Aladdin was not dead. He and Abu were in the palace dungeon. Yet all Aladdin could think about was Jasmine.

"She's a princess!" he said to himself. "She deserves a prince, not someone like me."

Just then an old man appeared from the shadows. It was Jafar in disguise. "I can help you get out of here and find treasures enough to impress your princess," he said, "if you will help me find a worthless old lamp."

Eager to escape, Aladdin agreed. Soon they were on their way to the Cave of Wonders.

When they got to the desert, Jafar fitted the scarab pieces together. At once the Cave of Wonders rose up from the sand.

"Touch nothing but the lamp," rumbled the Voice of the Cave.

"Quickly, my boy," urged the old man. "My lamp is in there. Fetch it, and you shall have your reward."

Aladdin and Abu entered the cave. In the first room they found gold and jewels – and a friendly Magic Carpet. The Carpet led them to another room and to the magic lamp. But just as Aladdin was about to grab the lamp, Abu reached for a giant ruby.

"No, Abu!" shouted Aladdin. But it was too late.

"You have touched the forbidden treasure!" thundered the Voice of the Cave. "Now you will never again see the light of day!"

All at once the cave walls began to crumble and the floor melted into a swirling pool of lava. Aladdin grabbed the lamp, but then he slipped! Before he fell into the fiery liquid, he was saved by the Magic Carpet. They rescued Abu and flew to the entrance of the cave.

Just as they reached the entrance, a boulder knocked the Magic Carpet out from under them. Aladdin fell off, but he managed to grasp the rim of the cave.

"Help!" he shouted to the old man. But instead of helping, Jafar took the lamp. Angrily, Abu jumped up and bit the old man.

"AGGH!" shrieked Jafar, throwing Abu into the cave. Aladdin could hold on no longer. The cave collapsed, sealing Aladdin and Abu deep inside it.

It was quiet when Aladdin awoke. "We're trapped!" he said to Abu and the Carpet.

To cheer him up, Abu pulled the lamp from his vest.

"Why, you little thief!" chuckled Aladdin, taking the lamp. "There's something written on it, but it's hard to read," he said as he rubbed the lamp.

The lamp began to glow. Then, in a puff of blue smoke, out popped a magical genie! "Say, you're a lot smaller than my last master," the Genie said.

"I'm your master?" asked Aladdin in surprise.

"That's right," replied the Genie. "I'm here for your wish fulfilment. You have three of them, to be exact – but no wishing for more wishes."

"I don't know," said Aladdin slyly. "You probably can't even get us out of this cave."

"You don't know?" said the Genie. "Well, watch this!"

Quick as a wink the Genie whisked them all out of the cave.

"Not bad," said Aladdin, "and I still have three wishes." The Genie laughed. "All right. But no more freebies!"

"What would you wish for?" Aladdin asked him.

"That's easy," said the Genie. "For my freedom. But my master has to wish for that – so you can guess how often that's happened."

Aladdin tried to imagine living inside a lamp. Then he said, "I'll use my third wish to set you free. But first I wish to be a prince," he added, as thoughts of Jasmine filled his head.

With a snap of his fingers the Genie
changed Aladdin's ragged clothes into
silken robes and Abu into a handsome
elephant.

"Now I am worthy of the Princess," said Aladdin happily as he put the lamp under his turban. It wasn't long before he was being ushered into the Sultan's palace.

"I am Prince Ali Ababwa," Aladdin declared. "I have come to win the hand of Princess Jasmine."

But Jasmine thought the young man was another silly prince, and she fled the room in disgust.

Later, Prince Ali managed to convince Jasmine to go for a midnight ride on the Magic Carpet.

"Is it safe?" she asked.

"Sure," he replied. "Do you trust me?"

In a flash, Jasmine remembered where she had heard those words before. "Yes," she said softly, taking his hand.

Jasmine stepped onto the Carpet and away they soared.

Could this prince be the boy I met in the marketplace? wondered Jasmine. She decided to find out.

"It's a shame Abu couldn't come with us," she said.

"Abu doesn't really like to fly," replied Aladdin.

"It *is* you!" blurted Jasmine.

But Aladdin was still too ashamed to admit he wasn't really a prince.

Aladdin and Jasmine enjoyed their romantic ride. Then they flew back to the palace and said goodnight with a kiss.

Meanwhile, Jafar had decided to marry Jasmine himself. So as soon as Jasmine was out of sight, the guards grabbed Aladdin.

"I'm afraid you have worn out your welcome, Prince Ali," Jafar hissed. Then the guards tied Aladdin up and threw him into the sea!

The weights attached to Aladdin's feet pulled him deep into the water. His turban fell off and the lamp tumbled out. He managed to rub it and the Genie appeared.

"Al! Snap out of it!" the Genie urged. "You have to say, 'Genie, I want you to save my life.' OK?"

Aladdin nodded slightly, and the Genie brought him to shore.

Back in the palace, Jafar had used his magical cobra staff to place the Sultan under a spell.

"Jasmine...you...will...marry... Jafar," droned the Sultan.

"Never!" cried Jasmine. "Father, I choose Prince Ali!"

At that moment Aladdin burst into the room. He broke Jafar's staff and shouted, "Your Highness, Jafar has been controlling you with this."

In the struggle Jafar spotted the magic lamp hidden in Aladdin's turban. As soon as Jafar escaped, he had Iago steal it. "So! Aladdin and Prince Ali are the same!" cried Jafar when he had the lamp at last.

Jafar eagerly rubbed the lamp and the Genie appeared. Jafar wished to be sultan. Then he wished to be a powerful sorcerer. He turned the Sultan into a jester, Jasmine into a slave and Rajah into a tiger cub.

"I am the most powerful man in the world!" Jafar declared.

"No, you're not!" shouted Aladdin. "The Genie is!"

"You're right," Jafar agreed. "The Genie's power does exceed my own. But not for long. My third wish is to be an all-powerful genie!"

"Your wish," said the Genie, "is my command."

In a flash Jafar grew into a mighty genie. But before he could enjoy his new powers, shackles appeared on his wrists and a lamp appeared beneath him. With a giant WHOOSH!!! he and Iago were sucked down into the tiny lamp!

"Ten thousand years in the Cave of Wonders ought to chill him out," said the Genie as he flung Jafar's lamp far into the desert. Everything returned to normal.

True to his word, Aladdin used his last wish to free the Genie. Then he turned to Jasmine and said softly, "I'm sorry I lied to you about being a prince."

"I know why you did," Jasmine answered.

"Prince or no prince, you've certainly proved your worth. It's the law that's the problem," declared the Sultan. "From this day on, the Princess shall marry whomever she deems worthy."

"I choose Aladdin," Jasmine said.

Everyone waved goodbye to the Genie as he flew off to see the world. Then Jasmine and Aladdin shared a gentle kiss – and lived happily ever after!